Stornoway Primary School
Jamieson Drive
Stornoway
Isle of Lewis
HS1 2LF
Tel: 01851 703418/703621
Fax: 01851 706257
Mail: stornoway-primary@cne-siar.gov.uk

This edition published by Parragon in 2013

Parragon
Chartist House
15–17 Trim Street
Bath BA1 1HA, UK
www.parragon.com

ISBN 978-1-4723-3096-3

Printed in China

Adapted by Michael Teitelbaum

Based on the teleplay "Day One, Part Two"

by Joshua Sternin and Jeffrey Ventimilia

CHAPTER 1

My name is Donatello, but you can call me Donnie. I'm a turtle.

Leonardo tells you in his story that, my brothers and I were inside the hideout of a strange species called the Kraang. We were there to rescue my girlfriend and the man with her, who is a scientist just like me.

Well, okay, she wasn't really my girlfriend – not yet, anyway.

But I was sure that once I learned her name and she got to know me, she would become my girlfriend. I felt it in my bones – we were meant to be together.

At that moment, the four of us were looking down at the inside of the Kraang's hideout.

Now, I was pretty familiar with just about every piece of technology humans have ever

invented, but the stuff I was seeing there – wow!
This was all super-high-tech alien equipment.
It wasn't even vaguely familiar to me.

Kraang guards were patrolling the entire area.
We hung on to the rafters and waited for the
right time to make our move. When all the guards
except two had disappeared, Leonardo and
Raphael dropped down and knocked them out.

Leo signalled to Mikey and me to join them. Up close, this place was even more incredible.

"Wow," I said to Raph. "I've never seen anything like this. They're using a metal alloy that even I don't recognize!"

"Gosh," Raph said in that mocking tone he uses whenever I talk tech. "A metal alloy even you don't know about. It boggles the mind!"

I really can't stand it when he talks to me that way. Especially since he doesn't know the first thing about metal alloys.

"Dude, you want to talk metallurgy with me?" I asked, getting up in Raph's face. "Bring it!"

"As a matter of fact, I don't want to have that conversation with you," Raph replied. "And–"

"Guys!" Leonardo interrupted. I could hear the frustration in his voice. "What part of being in an enemy lair do you not understand?"

Leo made a good point. Splinter always talked about ninjas using stealth and silence. I guess Raph and I weren't being too stealthy or silent-y.

I had to do a better job of focusing on the task at hand. We spotted a group of Kraang guards. Using the element of surprise, we easily subdued them. Then we sneaked into another room and got our first close-up look at these dudes.

Holy cow! Mikey was right!

The Kraang weren't wearing suits any more – in fact, they weren't even wearing skin! Their human appearances had only been a disguise.

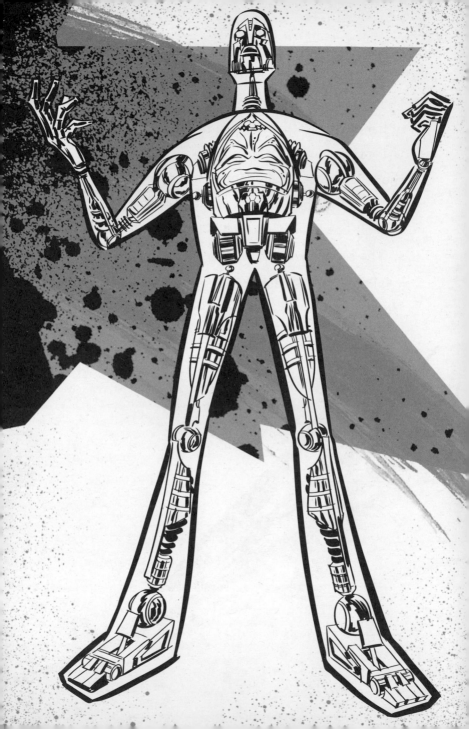

Underneath they seemed to be cybernetic robots of some sort. I couldn't tell what their blue outer armour was made of, but it was translucent, and I could see the pistons and motors working away underneath it. Their eyes were weird, glowing red lights.

Two thoughts hit me instantly: The first was, "Wow! I totally have to build a robot when I get back to the lair." And the second was, "Wow, Mikey was actually one hundred percent right about this one!"

"Alien robots!" I said. "They really are alien robots!"

"Alien robots, huh?" Mikey said, rubbing his chin. "Now, where have I heard that before? Oh, yeah, I remember. I've only been saying it since the first day we came above ground!"

The Kraangdroids attacked and we battled them. They fought furiously, blasting their energy weapons, but all our ninja training paid off.

One Kraangdroid had me in his sights. I rolled away, feeling the heat of the explosion on my back. I came up ready to lunge, hoping one good jab of my *bo* staff would get me a better look at his wiring.

The best thing was, we were finally working as a team, taking out the Kraang one by one.

Or so I thought.

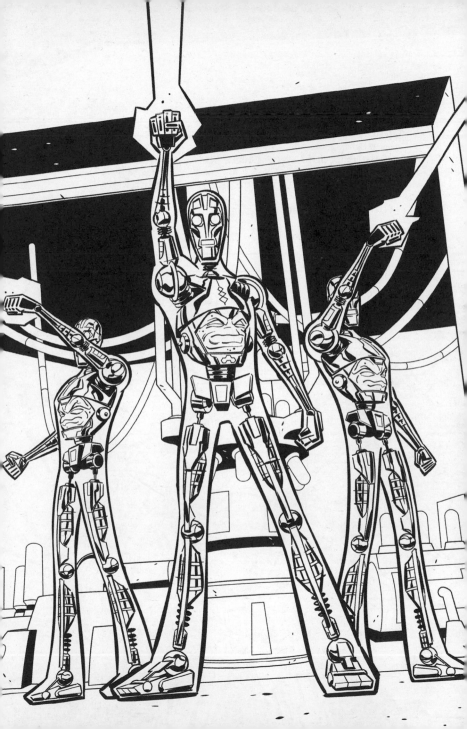

I glanced back over my shoulder and saw that one of the Kraang had backed Leo into a corner. Before I could even move to help him out, Leo tossed a handful of blinding powder into the robot's face. Then he sliced at its midsection with his *katana.*

The Kraangdroid tumbled backward and started sparking. Smoke poured from the opening in its belly. And then maybe the strangest thing I'd ever seen happened. No, there's no maybe about it – it *was* the strangest thing I'd ever seen.

A pink brain, with eyes and a mouth and whipping tentacles, slithered out of the opening.

Mikey reacted swiftly. He slammed the brain-thing with his *nunchucks,* stunning it. Then he picked up the slippery, slimy creature by one tentacle and shook it at the rest of us.

"See! See! I told you!" he shouted. "It's a brain-thing. I told you! I told you, but did any of you believe me? Nooooo . . . because you all think I'm just some kind of bonehead!"

That was when the stunned brain-thing woke up. It bit Mikey on the arm.

"Ow!" he cried, flinging the creature off himself.

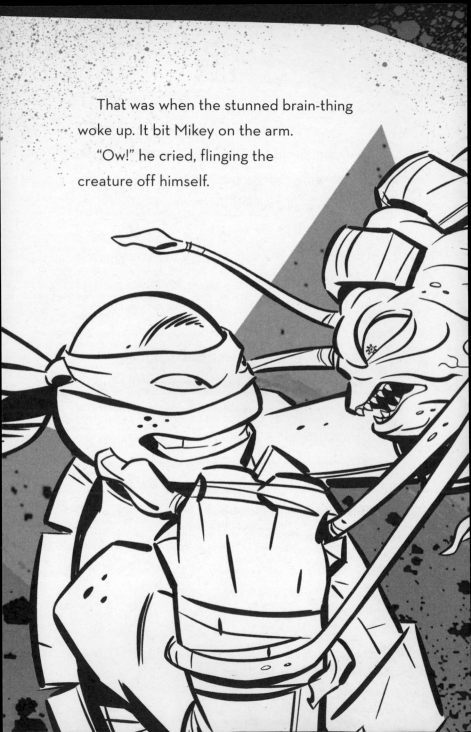

It flew across the room and slammed into an alarm button, setting off a loud, blaring siren. Not the best way to prove his point about not being a bonehead, in my humble opinion. My brothers and I all stared at Mikey.

"Okay, I know – bad move. But I was still right about the whole alien robot brain-thing!" he said defensively. "You've gotta give me that!"

Kraangdroids started appearing in every doorway and hall.

"Let's move!" Leonardo ordered.

"Move where?" Raph asked. He had a point. It seemed like the Kraangdroids were everywhere. I looked around, searching for a way out of this. Then I spotted something vaguely familiar overhead.

"I think those are power conduits," I said, looking up at the ceiling.

"That is really interesting," Raphael said, his voice dripping with sarcasm. "Thanks for sharing, Donnie!"

He thought I was just showing off, but he totally missed the point!

"Listen, meathead, the conduits are all converging that way," I explained, pointing to a corner where the pipes disappeared. "Which means that whatever is going on in that direction is important!"

I took off in the direction the conduits were heading. Leonardo ran close behind. Glancing back over my shoulder, I saw Mikey pointing a finger in Raph's face.

"You got spanked by Donnie!" he said, laughing loudly.

Raph didn't answer. He just grabbed Mikey's finger and bent it backwards.

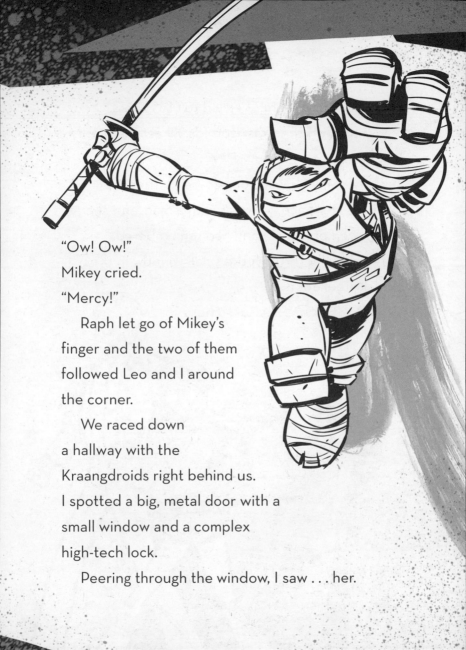

"Ow! Ow!"
Mikey cried.
"Mercy!"

Raph let go of Mikey's
finger and the two of them
followed Leo and I around
the corner.

We raced down
a hallway with the
Kraangdroids right behind us.
I spotted a big, metal door with a
small window and a complex
high-tech lock.

Peering through the window, I saw . . . her.

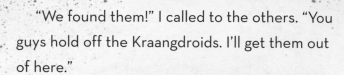

"We found them!" I called to the others. "You guys hold off the Kraangdroids. I'll get them out of here."

It was my almost, soon-to-be girlfriend, What's-Her-Face. She was with a man, and she was even prettier than I had remembered. I stared at her through the small window in the thick steel door.

"Don't worry," I assured her.

"I'll have you out of there in a second!"

"Okay, giant lizard-thing," the girl replied.

OK, so she wasn't so clear on our species. But I could tell we were totally making progress – this time she didn't shriek when she saw my face!

"Turtle, actually," I pointed out. "I'm Donatello."

I couldn't believe I was finally getting the chance to introduce myself to her properly. This was so exciting!

"April," she replied.

April . . . hmmm . . .

"Wow, that's a pretty na–"

Laser pulses bounced off the hallway walls.

"The lock, Donnie!" Leonardo shouted, pressing my face into the glass.

"Right! Sorry! The lock."

I got right to work rewiring the circuitry, but it was slow going. I could hear Mikey attack a line of Kraangdroids with spinning blows from his *nunchucks.* The robots went down like bowling pins. Inside the cell, April was starting to panic.

"Not to rush you or anything," she said, "but hurry up!"

"Hey!" I shot back. "You think it's easy trying to pick a lock with these hands?" I held up my three thick fingers so April could see them clearly through the glass.

"Oh, sorry," April replied.

Aww, she was so sweet!

Raphael stepped up to the door.

"Oh, for the love of– Get out of my way!" he shouted, shoving me away from the door.

Raphael attacked the electronic lock with his
sais. Again and again he jammed the sharp points
into the delicate mechanism. Sparks flew. But
before he could force the door open, another

door at the back of the cell slid back. A group of Kraangdroids grabbed April and the man and dragged them from the cell.

"No! No! Let me go!" April shouted, as she disappeared. Just as Raph finally got the door to open and we raced into the cell, a Kraangdroid jumped up behind us. Raph slammed the door shut on the thing's arm, tearing it from its socket. He slipped the robot arm through the door handles to keep any more Kraangdroids from joining our little party.

"That'll hold 'em," Raph said. A loud banging came from the other side of the door.

"But not for long!"

The robot arm twitched and smoked.

I couldn't believe what I'd just seen.

"Raph, you are seriously twisted," Leonardo said.

"Thank you," said Raph.

We took off after April and the man. We followed the winding halls out of the building and eventually came out onto the courtyard.

"Help!" came a cry from a walkway above. I looked up and spotted April and the man being hurried away by some Kraangdroids.

"Let's get them!" Leonardo shouted.

"Uh-oh," Mikey said. He looked really freaked out. As I spun around, I saw a terrifying sight – it was a giant human-weed mutant thing waving its sharp, green leaves at us, ready to strike!

The weed-man stared down at us and growled. Actually, it was more like a hiss. Or was it a squeal? Well, whatever, he was not happy to see us.

"It's Snake!" Leonardo cried. "He's mutated into a . . . a . . . giant weed!"

Snake hissed (or growled, or whatever) at us again.

"That's weird," Mikey said. "You'd think he'd mutate into a snake."

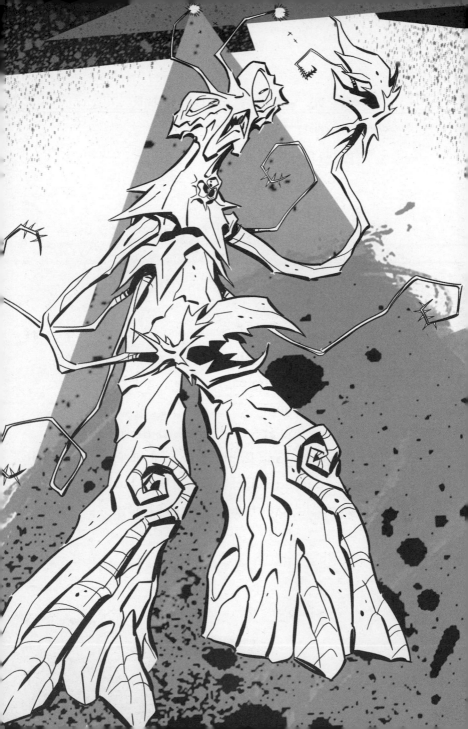

"Yeah, you would," Raph said to Mikey, "if you were an idiot!"

"But his name is Snake," Mikey said, explaining his own peculiar brand of logic.

"So?" Raph asked.

Mikey shook his head in frustration. "You just don't understand science." As someone who does understand science, I just have to laugh at Mikey sometimes.

"You did this to me!" Snake hissed, from the green, leafy opening that had once been his human mouth. Technically he was right, but he did have it coming.

Snake swiped at us with a sharp, thorny vine, knocking Mikey and Raph off their feet. Leo spun and ducked out of the way, then flashed his sword and sliced a stalk off Snake's body.

Green, gloppy goo poured out of the weed-man's wound, splashing all over Mikey.

"Ewww!" Mikey yelled. He jumped and twitched, desparately trying to wipe off the slop.

I stared in amazement at the weed-man. The vine that Leo had sliced off was slowly beginning to grow back!

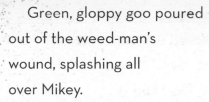

"It grew back?" I shouted. "No fair!"

The weed-man attacked us again. In the distance I heard a faint sound. It was kind of familiar, like something I had heard before on TV, but I couldn't quite place it. Some sort of machine was making a THAP-THAP-THAP-THAP noise.

Leo knew what it was right away.

"Donnie!" he shouted, pointing in the direction of the sound. "Go!"

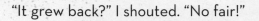

There was no time to hesitate. I sprinted toward the sound, leaving my brothers to battle the weed-man.

"Snakeweed is really hard to kill!" I heard Mikey say.

"Snakeweed?" Raph asked.

"Yeah!" Mikey replied. "His name was Snake and now he's a weed, so–"

"We get it! Just keep fighting!" Raph shouted.

"We just have to hold it off until Donnie gets back!" I heard Leo say.

The pressure was squarely on me. I rounded a corner and saw what was making the noise. It was a helicopter. Its blades spun around and around, faster and faster. Then I spotted them – April and the man being forced into the helicopter by a group of Kraangdroids.

The helicopter started to lift off the ground. No! I had to do something.

Thinking fast, I used my *bo* staff like a vaulting pole to launch myself into the air.

I landed on one of the helicopter's long, metal skids and then hung on for dear life as it rose into the sky.

In the courtyard below, I saw my brothers battling Snakeweed. Suddenly, Leo broke away from the others and ran across to the other side. I wondered where he was heading. Then I saw it. He was racing to the power generator at the end of all those conduits. Way to go, Leo!

Just then, the door to the helicopter slid open and a Kraangdroid leaned out. It aimed its energy weapon at me and started blasting away.

I had to move quickly. I dodged the energy blasts, using the skid as a shield. The Kraangdroid leaned out farther. He was trying to get a better angle for a shot at me. That was when I remembered something Splinter had taught us. He told us to always use our opponent's movement and position against him.

My next move was obvious. I reached up, grabbed the Kraangdroid's wrist, and yanked hard. He came tumbling out of the helicopter to the ground below.

However, as a scientist, I should have remembered that every action has an equal and opposite reaction. The sudden change in weight caused the helicopter to lurch to the side. April fell out of the open door.

"Yiiiiii!" she screamed, grabbing the metal skid.

"Hold on! I'm coming!" I shouted.

But April lost her grip and plummeted toward the ground! I don't remember thinking anything in particular, I just remember knowing that I couldn't lose her. And I knew exactly what I had to do. I let go of the skid and dropped to the ground, using all my ninja training to land safely. I hit the ground a split second before April. Rolling up on to my feet, I reached out and caught her in my arms.

"You okay?" I asked, as she looked around and tried to catch her breath.

She stared up at me and nodded. Then her eyes opened wide and she looked up at the helicopter, which still held the man, as it sped off into the sky.

I felt really bad for her. I wished I could have saved the man, too!

April and I stepped out into the courtyard. Across the way, I saw Raph and Mikey hacking away at Snakeweed's leafy limbs. Then I spotted a platoon of Kraangdroids marching toward my brothers, firing their energy weapons.

Something weird was going on here. Raph and Mikey were pushing Snakeweed toward the power generator where Leo waited.

"What are they doing?" I wondered. "They're leading Snakeweed right to the power generator! That's really dangerous – and incredibly stupid! If one of those Kraangdroid energy blasts were to hit the generator – KA-BOOM!"

Or maybe . . .

"Or it's incredibly brilliant!" I said to April, who was looking at me like I had just landed from outer space. "Or it's both!"

I watched as Snakeweed came closer and closer to Leonardo, who stood just a few feet from the generator.

"Come and get me, Stinkweed!" Leo taunted.

Snakeweed raised itself up to its full height, reached back with a sharp, viney tentacle, and brought it down right toward Leo's head.

But my brother was ready.

Leo did a backflip and landed directly on top of the generator. Then Leo made funny faces at the Kraangdroids. At that moment I understood Leo's plan. It was brilliant, after all.

The Kraangdroids opened fire on Leo, who jumped off the power generator just in time.

The Kraangdroids' energy blasts slammed into the generator. Powerful bolts of electricity shot from the power source and wrapped themselves around Snakeweed.

Snakeweed went up in a shower of sparks and flames. He shrieked hideously, then collapsed in a heap of burnt plant pieces.

"Turtles, move!" Leo shouted.

The fire and smoke gave us the cover we needed to get the heck out of there! My brothers and I, along with April, ran from the hideout.

As I left the building, I overheard the Kraangdroids talking.

"Kraang, the ones in this place are not in this place where they were," said one Kraangdroid.

"The ones are called Turtles, Kraang," said another. "They are dangerous to what we are doing in this place. And other places."

"Yes, I am knowledge of that," said the first. "The Turtles must be eliminated from all places."

With all that sophisticated robotic technology, you'd think they'd have better vocal-processing software, right? I don't know why they needed so many words to say they were going to get rid of us. But I did know one thing – we had made our first deadly enemies.

CHAPTER 3

Once we got away from the Kraangdroids'
hideout, I asked April where she planned to go,
since the man, who turned out to be her father,
was still a prisoner.

She explained that her aunt lived in the city
and that they were very close. So we went with
April to her aunt's apartment.

Sitting on the roof of her aunt's building, I was worried about April. She seemed so sad. She missed her father so much.

"Are you going to be all right?" I asked her.

"I guess," she said quietly, shrugging. "My aunt says I can stay here as long as I want. But I'll be a lot better when I track down the creeps that took my dad."

"Won't the police help?" Leonardo asked.

April grimaced. "Funny thing," she said. "When you tell them your dad was kidnapped by alien brains in robot bodies, they don't take you all that seriously."

"I hear that," Mikey said.

I wanted so badly to be able to save the day for her. "April," I said, "I promise you we will not rest until we find him."

Raphael looked startled. "We won't?" he said, sounding genuinely surprised.

Leo elbowed Raph. "No, April. We won't," he said. And that is why Leo, not Raph, is our leader!

"Thank you," April said, sighing. "But it's not your fight."

I reached out and took April's hand into mine.

"Yes," I said softly, "it is."

April looked into my eyes, and for the first time since we met, smiled at me.

I'm pretty sure I won't ever forget that smile. But all too soon, the moment was over. April went back inside her aunt's flat, and my brothers and I climbed down off the roof and disappeared into the darkness.

We went back to our lair. Mikey, Raph, and I flipped on the TV and settled in to relax after our big adventure. I felt glad that we had finally gotten out of the lair and into the world. But I was still worried about April.

Leonardo went to meet in private with Master Splinter. I guess that's what happens when you're the leader. But I really wanted to know what they were saying, in case it had to do with April. So don't tell Leo, but I did a little eavesdropping with a nifty gizmo I had made a while ago, out of some spare electronics.

"I am impressed, Leonardo," Splinter was saying. "You proved to be an effective leader under the most difficult of circumstances."

"Thank you, *Sensei*," Leo said. "And I think I figured out why you made me leader."

"Oh? Why is that?" Splinter asked.

"Because you sensed inside me a true warrior's spirit that could forge us all into the heroes we are destined to become."

Leonardo was sounding pretty full of himself.

"No," Splinter replied.

"No?" Leo asked, confused. "Then why did you make me leader?"

"Because you asked."

"That's it?" Leo said. Now he was sounding like someone had stuck a pin in his balloon. "But you seemed so certain you were right."

"As a leader, you will learn that there is no right or wrong," Splinter explained. "There are only choices."

54

"So you could have chosen any of us?" Leo asked in a sad little voice.

"Yes."

"Even Mikey?"

"No, that would have been wrong," Splinter said quickly.

Just then, Mikey called us all over to the television set. "Everybody! Come here!" he shouted excitedly. "Check it out – we made the news! We're on TV!"

Splinter and Leo joined us in the common area to watch.

"There has been a report of – get this – ninjas in New York," the newscaster was saying. "Don't believe me? After residents reported a disturbance, the police recovered this." The screen showed a picture of one of our ninja throwing stars!

"This is so awesome!" Mikey cried. "We are gonna be famous!"

Splinter scowled. Then he spoke. "You must be more careful!" he said sternly.

Whoa! I didn't expect that. He seemed kind of upset with us.

"The ninja's most powerful weapon is the shadows," he explained. "Being brought out into the light is a dangerous thing."

"Relax, *Sensei*," Raphael said. "It's one little news story. What's the worst that can happen?"

I guess we should all have been very worried. After all, there was an army of alien robots mad at us and we were in danger of being revealed on the news.

But I had to admit, I was feeling pretty good. I almost, sort of had a girlfriend. And even more amazing, my brothers and I were really awesome ninjas. We weren't just playing in our rooms anymore. We'd been on a real mission and kicked some serious shell.

I knew I'd do anything for my brothers, and
I was sure they'd always watch my shell.

We were a truly epic team!

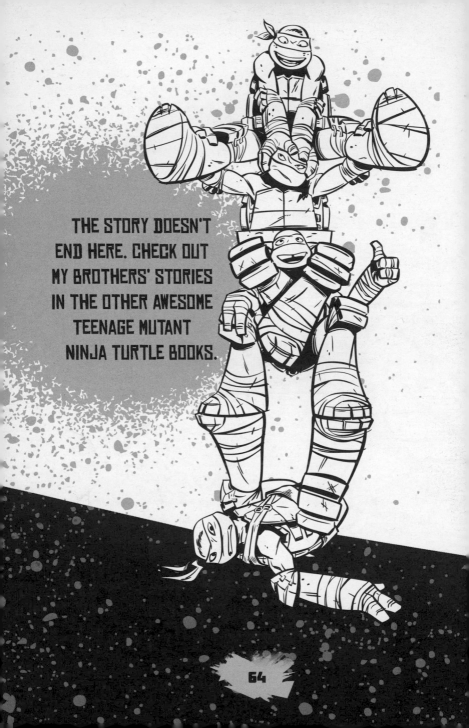

THE STORY DOESN'T
END HERE. CHECK OUT
MY BROTHERS' STORIES
IN THE OTHER AWESOME
TEENAGE MUTANT
NINJA TURTLE BOOKS.

DONATELLO

Donatello is the team's brilliant inventor.
He can make amazing gadgets, weapons,
and vehicles from just about anything he
can find. Donnie's brothers think he's a bit
of a nerd, but they also know they can
always rely on him to find a clever way
out of any tricky situation.

NAGINATA

Though Donatello can make any weapon he wants, nothing compares to his *naginata*. This is a long fighting *bo* staff with a blade at the end.

The Pursuit of the
Ivory Poachers:
KENYA

KT-162-004

Join Secret Agent Jack Stalwart

on his other adventures:

The Search for the Sunken Treasure: **AUSTRALIA**

The Secret of the Sacred Temple: **CAMBODIA**

The Mystery of the Mona Lisa: **FRANCE**

The Caper of the Crown Jewels: **GREAT BRITAIN**

The Escape of the Deadly Dinosaur: **USA**

The Pursuit
of the
Ivory Poachers:
KENYA

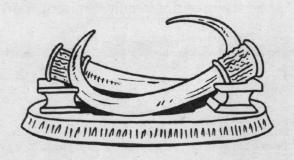

Elizabeth Singer Hunt

Illustrated by Brian Williamson

RED FOX

THE PURSUIT OF THE IVORY POACHERS: KENYA
A RED FOX BOOK 978 1 849 41823 2

First published in Great Britain by Red Fox,
an imprint of Random House Children's Publishers UK

This edition published 2007

2

Printed and bound in Great Britain by Clays Ltd, St Ives plc

Set in Meta, Trixie, American Typewriter, Luggagetag,
Gill Sans Condensed and Serpentine.

Red Fox Books are published by Random House Children's Publishers UK
61–63 Uxbridge Road, London W5 5SA
A Random House Group Company

www.**randomhousechildrens**.co.uk

Addresses for companies within The Random House Group can be found at
www.randomhouse.co.uk/offices.htm

THE RANDOM HOUSE GROUP Limited Reg. No. 954009

A CIP catalogue record for this book is available from the British Library.

For my parents, who, like me,
love the African plains

Destination:
KENYA

JACK STALWART

Jack Stalwart applied to be a secret
agent for the Global Protection
Force four months ago.

My name is Jack Stalwart. My older brother,

Max, was a secret agent for you, until he

disappeared on one of your missions. Now I

want to be a secret agent too. If you choose

me, I will be an excellent secret agent and get

rid of evil villains, just like my brother did.

Sincerely,

Jack Stalwart

Jack Stalwart was sworn in as a Global Protection Force secret agent four months ago. Since that time, he has completed all of his missions successfully and has stopped no less than twelve evil villains. Because of this he has been assigned the code name 'COURAGE'.

Jack has yet to uncover the whereabouts of his brother, Max, who is still working for this organization at a secret location. Do not give Secret Agent Jack Stalwart this information. He is never to know about his brother.

Gerald Barter
Director, Global Protection Force

THINGS YOU'LL FIND IN EVERY BOOK

 **Watch Phone:** The only gadget Jack wears all the time, even when he's not on official business. His Watch Phone is the central gadget that makes most others work. There are lots of important features, most importantly the 'C' button, which reveals the code of the day – necessary to unlock Jack's Secret Agent Book Bag. There are buttons on both sides, one of which ejects his life-saving Melting Ink Pen. Beyond these functions, it also works as a phone and, of course, gives Jack the time of day.

 **Global Protection Force (GPF):** The GPF is the organization Jack works for. It's a worldwide force of young secret agents whose aim is to protect the world's people, places and possessions. No one knows exactly where its main offices are located (all correspondence and gadgets for repair are sent to a special PO Box, and training is held at various locations around the world), but Jack thinks it's somewhere cold, like the Arctic Circle.

Whizzy: Jack's magical miniature globe. Almost every night at precisely 7:30 p.m., the GPF uses Whizzy to send Jack the identity of the country that he must travel to. Whizzy can't talk, but he can cough up messages. Jack's parents don't know Whizzy is anything more than a normal globe.

The Magic Map: The magical map hanging on Jack's bedroom wall. Unlike most maps, the GPF's map is made of a mysterious wood. Once Jack inserts the country piece from Whizzy, the map swallows Jack whole and sends him away on his missions. When he returns, he arrives precisely one minute after he left.

Secret Agent Book Bag: The Book Bag that Jack wears on every adventure. Licensed only to GPF secret agents, it contains top-secret gadgets necessary to foil bad guys and escape certain death. To activate the bag before each mission, Jack must punch in a secret code given to him by his Watch Phone. Once he's away, all he has to do is place his finger on the zip, which identifies him as the owner of the bag and immediately opens.

THE STALWART FAMILY

Jack's dad, John

He moved the family to England when Jack was two, in order to take a job with an aerospace company. As far as Jack knows, his dad designs and manufactures aeroplane parts. Jack's dad thinks he is an ordinary boy and that his other son, Max, attends a school in Switzerland. Jack's dad is American and his mum is British, which makes Jack a bit of both.

Jack's mum, Corinne

One of the greatest mums as far as Jack is concerned. When she and her husband received a letter from a posh school in Switzerland inviting Max to attend, they were overjoyed. Since Max left six months ago, they have received numerous notes in Max's handwriting telling them he's OK. Little do they know it's all a lie and that it's the GPF sending those letters.

Jack's older brother, Max

Two years ago, at the age of nine, Max joined the GPF. Max used to tell Jack about his adventures and show him how to work his secret-agent gadgets. When the family received a letter inviting Max to attend a school in Europe, Jack figured it was to do with the GPF. Max told him he was right, but that he couldn't tell Jack anything about why he was going away.

Nine-year-old Jack Stalwart

Four months ago, Jack received an anonymous note saying: 'Your brother is in danger. Only you can save him.' As soon as he could, Jack applied to be a secret agent too. Since that time, he's battled some of the world's most dangerous villains, and hopes some day in his travels to find and rescue his brother, Max.

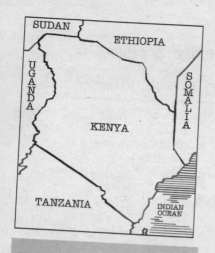

DESTINATION:
Kenya

The sun rises at 7:00 a.m. and sets at 7:00 p.m. every day in Kenya because it's on the equator

•

Kenya is on the continent of Africa, the second largest continent in the world

•

Nairobi is its capital city

•

Kenya is a country with beaches, snow-capped mountains and world-famous safari parks

The Rift Valley, also called the 'Cradle of Mankind', runs through Kenya. It's where many scientists believe 'early man' first evolved and lived

•

Although Swahili is the national language, many people speak English

The Great Travel Guide

ELEPHANTS: FACTS AND FIGURES

The word elephant means 'great arch'

Elephants are the largest land mammals in the world. They can grow to be four metres tall and weigh 5,400 kilograms

There are two kinds of elephants: African and Asian or Indian

Elephants have twenty-six teeth, including their tusks. Tusks are made of ivory and have been sought after by hunters for thousands of years

Elephants can live to be seventy years old. The main threat to their survival is poaching by man. During the 1970s and 1980s, more than eighty per cent of Kenya's elephant population was killed for its ivory

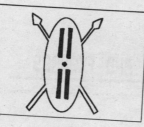

CULTURAL FILE:
The Maasai

The Maasai are a tribe of semi-nomadic people living in eastern Africa

•

There are roughly 350,000 Maasai living in Kenya

•

They survive by herding and trading cows, goats and sheep with other families

Maasai live on homesteads. Their homes are made of mud, sticks, grass, cow poo and urine

SECRET AGENT PHRASEBOOK FOR KENYA (SWAHILI)

SECRET AGENT GADGET INSTRUCTION MANUAL

Hydro Pills: The GPF's Hydro
Pills are an essential gadget for any
secret agent working in extreme heat.
Just shake two pills onto the tip of
your tongue. Instantly, a burst of
fresh water will fill your mouth. Swallow it and feel
refreshed.

Transformation Dust:

When you need to change your
appearance, even for a short while,
use the GPF's Transformation Dust.
Open the green packet and sprinkle
some dust onto your head. At the same time, say what
you want to become out loud. Within seconds, you will
be transformed. To use on other people, just blow the
dust over them for the same effect. Consult the back of
this handbook for a complete list of transformation
options.

Anti-Intruder Alarm:

The GPF's Anti-Intruder Alarm is the best way to guard against intruders. To activate it, just select the 'AI' mode on your Watch Phone. The gadget will scan the surrounding area for up to five metres and send a vibration to your wrist if someone or something is detected.

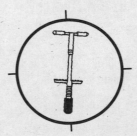

Power Pogo:

When you need to jump farther than your feet will take you, use the GPF's Power Pogo. The Power Pogo looks like an ordinary pogo stick, but it can catapult you up to five metres into the air. Perfect when you need to get out of harm's way. Just step on and jump.

Chapter 1:
The Letter

It was a warm summer evening and Jack and his mum were sitting at the kitchen table together. Jack's dad, John, was busy at work and wouldn't be home until later that night. As Jack took a bite of his cottage pie, his mum perked up with a bit of news.

'Did I tell you that we got a letter from Max?' she asked Jack.

'Really?' said Jack, only mildly interested. He figured it was another GPF letter designed to make his parents think Max was at a school in Switzerland instead of on an assignment.

'It's over here,' she said, jumping up from the table and going into the lounge. As she rifled through the post, she went on to explain: 'And what's strange is that it's not from Switzerland. It's all the way from Egypt.'

'Egypt?' said Jack, nearly choking on a piece of carrot. Why would the GPF fake a letter from Egypt? he wondered. They usually sent Max's letters from an address in Switzerland.

As he was thinking about it, Jack's mum began to read the letter aloud.

'Dear Mum, Dad and JAck,

You won't Believe iT, but I'M on a field trip iN Egypt. We're learNing about the History of This greAt coUntry and Seeing all Of the anciEnt monumEnts.

Please Tell JacK I miss Him.

Lots of love,

Max'

'Isn't that sweet?' said Jack's mum. She was obviously proud of Max for making an effort to learn about the culture of a foreign country. 'And see how busy he is,' she added, pointing to the letter. 'He must have typed this really quickly.'

Jack walked over to his mum and peered at the note. There was a curious mix of upper-case and lower-case letters.

'Can I borrow the letter, Mum?' he asked, trying to hide his excitement.

'Of course, sweetheart,' she said. 'But take care of it. I'm saving all Max's letters for his special "Switzerland scrapbook".'

Before his mum could start talking again, Jack took the note and ran towards the stairs.

'Thanks!' he shouted as he climbed them two at a time. He reached his bedroom door and dashed inside to his bed. Climbing on top of his duvet, Jack stared carefully at the note.

It *looked* like a genuine letter. The way it was worded made it sound like Max. And the scribble at the end looked like Max's signature. But two things struck Jack as odd. Except for the handwritten signature, it was created by a typewriter instead of a computer and there was something going on with the size of some of the letters.

Jack reached under his bed and pulled out his Secret Agent Book Bag. Using his Watch Phone, he made contact with the GPF. Whenever a secret agent needed to use his or her gadgets when not on a mission, they could ask the GPF for special permission. Sure enough, the GPF quickly sent back the code SUPER CAR.

Jack laughed at how funny that was. He and his brother, Max, loved super cars like Ferraris and Lamborghinis.

Once Jack had entered the code, the lock popped open. He reached inside and grabbed his Signature ID. The Signature ID was a three-dimensional rectangular box with a silver viewing screen inside. It was the only gadget in the world that could analyse someone's handwriting and identify its creator from a worldwide file. Whenever a secret agent needed to figure out whether an important document – like a ransom note or an ownership paper – was forged, they used the Signature ID.

For Max's other letters, Louise Persnall was the name given by the Signature ID. Jack knew that Louise was personal secretary to the GPF Director, Gerald Barter. Hoping that this time the letter was for real, Jack crossed his fingers and placed the box over the note.

Patiently, he waited for the Signature ID to do its work. When it was finished, he heard it beep. He took a deep breath and looked down at the screen. When he read what was there, his heart skipped a beat.

CREATOR: MAXWELL JOHN STALWART

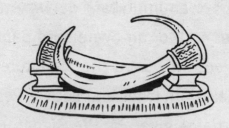

Chapter 2:
The Code

Jack's insides were really churning now. He quickly put the Signature ID back in his Book Bag. Aside from an anonymous note telling Jack that Max was in trouble, he'd received no other communication about his brother in the past six months.

Jack took another look at the note and studied the upper-case letters that shouldn't have been there. He grabbed a pen and paper from his bedside table and wrote them down. There weren't many

bigger letters, so maybe they formed
some sort of code.

ABTMNNHTAUSOEETKH

Hmm, Jack thought as he stared at the
jumble of letters. There was nothing
obvious about anything to do with his
brother.

When Jack was on a mission in Cambodia, he had received a clue about Max. His brother was supposedly working near a mummy in Egypt. After that tip, Jack did loads of research on mummies, but he still didn't have enough information to pinpoint Max's exact location.

Now, thought Jack as he stared at the code, he had been given a second chance. He was pretty sure that deep within the code was *where* Max was and *why* he was there. If Jack could solve it, he could probably help his brother. If he couldn't . . . well, Jack didn't even want to think about that.

Chapter 3:
The Assignment

Just then, Whizzy started to spin. Startled,
Jack looked at the clock next to his little
globe. It was already 7:30 p.m.

Before Jack could think any more about
Max, Whizzy coughed – Ahem! – and spat
a jigsaw piece out of his mouth. Leaving
his notes behind, Jack raced over to the
spot where it landed. He looked at it
carefully as he picked it up.

'Now where does this one fit?' he
asked, carrying the piece to his Magic

11

Map. The wooden map of the world that
hung on Jack's wall magically transported
him away on his missions when he fitted
the correct country into it.

He lifted the piece up to the left of the
map and tried to match it to Alaska.
When that didn't work, he moved it to
Canada. Going south through North

America and towards Mexico, he waited
for it to slot in, but it didn't fit. He carried
on, sliding the piece over South America,
but still no joy.

Wondering whether the country he was going to was actually Egypt, he picked up the piece and placed it over that country on the map. When it didn't match, he slid it over central Africa and towards the continent's eastern edge. When he reached the coast, the piece fell in. The name 'KENYA' appeared and then disappeared into the map.

'Kenya?' said Jack. He knew that Kenya was a place for safari holidays. Maybe a tourist is in trouble, he thought as he grabbed his Book Bag. He dialled into his Watch Phone for the code of the day. As soon as he received the word – S-A-F-A-R-I – he punched it into the bag's lock and it popped open. Looking through the contents, he made a mental note of his Hydro Pills, Flyboard and the Lava Laser.

Jack stuffed Max's note into his Book

Bag and zipped it shut. He raced back to the Magic Map, where the light inside Kenya was starting to grow. Knowing that he needed to be focused, Jack thought about Max one more time before sending worries about him out of his head.

When the orange light coming from the African country had filled his room, Jack yelled, 'Off to Kenya!' Then the light burst, swallowing him into the Magic Map.

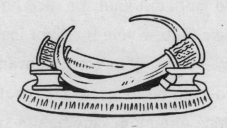

Chapter 4:
The Savannah

When Jack arrived, he found himself alone in an open field. The tall grass under his feet was brown and dry. There was a khaki-coloured dirt road to his far right, and the lone tree ahead was just that – all by itself.

From the looks of it, Jack figured he was in the savannah, one of the many types of land in Africa. Besides savannahs, Africa also had deserts and tropical rainforests, each with its own kind of exciting wildlife.

Jack opened his Book Bag and pulled out his Google Goggles. The GPF's Google Goggles looked like ordinary swim goggles but they enabled the wearer to see great distances both under the water and on land. He switched them to 'maximum' length, held them up to his eyes and waited for his vision to cut through the air.

Far in the distance he could see the animals of the plain. There was a herd of wildebeest making their way across a distant road. Beyond them was a family of giraffe. They were using their long tongues to eat leaves from some prickly branches. An ostrich leaped into view and dashed across the savannah.

Scanning with Google Goggles a further thirty degrees round, Jack noticed a group of gazelle, a small deer-like animal. They were busy eating something off the ground, while a group of patient lions watched their every move.

Jack looked at his Watch Phone. It had already adjusted itself to Kenyan time. Thankfully, it was after midday. Knowing that lions typically hunted in the cooler hours of the morning and night, Jack wiped the sweat from his brow. The last thing he needed was an encounter with a pack of hungry wild animals.

Chapter 5:
The Bungling Brit

WHOOSH!

All of a sudden, there was a noise from above.

WHOOSH!

There it was again.

Jack dropped to his knees and aimed his Google Goggles at the sky. Sailing towards him was a red, yellow and blue striped hot-air balloon. Hanging underneath the balloon was an enormous wicker basket, and in the basket was a man wearing a floppy hat.

'Hello!' The man waved to Jack from his perch inside the balloon. Jack thought he sounded English.

'Hello!' he shouted again. His arms were flapping wildly as he tried to gain control of the flying balloon. 'I'm not very good with this thing!' he yelled as the balloon jolted up and down in the sky. 'I say,' he went on. 'Is your name Jack?'

Jack took a quick look around. Since there wasn't anyone else for miles, he figured it was all right to say his name out loud. 'Yes!' he shouted back.

'Jolly good!' the man replied. 'I'd hate to have flown all this way to find out your name was Frank!' At this silly joke, he started roaring with laughter.

Jack watched the man try to steer the balloon to just above where he was standing. With a pull of a cord, he slowly lowered the craft. But instead of landing

gently, the balloon's basket hit the
ground and tipped over sideways.

'Arghhh!' the man screamed, tumbling
out onto the dry grass.

'Are you OK?' asked Jack as he moved quickly to help the man. He was trying not to laugh, but the whole thing was very funny.

'Absolutely!' said the man, jumping to his feet. He straightened his hat, quickly brushing the dirt from his trousers. 'Just a bit more practice and I'll have this balloon thing cracked! But where are my manners?' he exclaimed. 'Trevor Dimbleby.' He thrust out his hand. 'Nice to meet you.'

'Nice to meet you too, Trevor,' said Jack, shaking the pilot's hand. 'What seems to be the problem?' he asked, anxious to hear the reason for his mission.

'It's Chief Abasi who sent for you,' said Trevor. 'He's the one with the problem.'

'Chief Abasi?' asked Jack, curious to know who he was.

'Chief Abasi,' Trevor explained, 'is the chief of the local Maasai. He controls the

bit of the Maasai Mara where my boss
and I run a safari lodge.'

Jack knew that the Maasai Mara was
one of the biggest safari parks in Kenya
and that the Maasai were a group of
tribal people who lived off the land.

'Why don't we get a wriggle on?' said
Trevor, glancing at his watch. 'It's two
o'clock and I told the chief that I'd have
you back in half an hour.'

'Sure thing,' said Jack. 'But how are we
getting there?'

Trevor paused and smiled.

Jack looked at the balloon. 'You're
joking,' he said, not entirely confident
with Trevor's piloting skills.

'Don't be a scaredy-cat,' said Trevor as
he started walking towards the craft.

Knowing that he had a few gadgets to
help him out, Jack joined Trevor, who was
adjusting the temperature of the air, so

that the balloon could lift off the ground.

'Climb in!' he said to Jack.

Jack grabbed the edge of the basket
and pulled himself over the side. He
found a space next to the propane gas
tanks and watched as Trevor yanked on a
lever. A huge plume of flames shot up
above Jack's head and they started to
take off. Trevor tugged on the control

again and the balloon began to rise even higher.

As they climbed into the sky, they caught a current of wind. The balloon flew upwards and to the east, taking Jack and Trevor to Chief Abasi and the mission ahead.

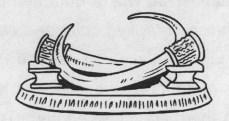

Chapter 6:
The Homestead

After about twenty minutes, Trevor nudged Jack and pointed to something on the ground. 'See that homestead over there?' he said. 'That's where we're heading.'

Jack lifted his Google Goggles once again, and surveyed the area around the village. There were five little homes made out of mud, a few small buildings and three fenced-off pens for keeping cattle. Children were playing games, while the women were busy with their chores. The entire homestead was surrounded by a thorny fence. It looked quiet and calm; not the kind of place that needed the services of an international secret agent.

When they were close enough, Trevor pulled a string to open the parachute valve. The parachute valve was on top of the balloon. It worked to let the hot air out, so the balloon would drop slowly to the ground. This time when the basket hit the earth, it did so gently. As it tipped over, Jack rolled out and Trevor followed him.

'So, where to now?' asked Jack, standing up.

'Over there,' said Trevor, pointing to the gate. 'Why don't you go on ahead? I need to stay here and pack up the balloon.'

As Jack walked through the gate and into the enclosure, he saw an African man coming out of one of the huts. He was wearing a red Maasai cloth around his shoulders, and some ornamental beads hung from his head and neck. With the aid of a wooden walking stick, he slowly made his way over to Jack. Figuring this was Chief Abasi, Jack extended his hand to greet him.

'*Jambo*,' said Jack. He knew that '*jambo*' meant hello in Swahili. '*Jina langu ni* Jack Stalwart.'

The chief broke into an enormous smile. He was obviously pleased by Jack's attempt to speak the Kenyan language.

Although the Maasai had a language of their own, the man understood enough of what Jack had said to respond.

'Welcome,' he said, 'to my homestead and to my country. I am honoured that you have come.' Jack was impressed by Chief Abasi's English. He was obviously a well-educated man.

Before Jack could ask, the chief got to the point. 'The reason I have called for you is that I have discovered a great problem on the Mara.'

'What's wrong?' Jack asked. He was wondering what could be so bad in such a peaceful place.

'Why don't we take a walk?' the chief said, motioning for Jack to follow him out of the homestead. 'Walking helps to clear my head,' he added.

Jack paused, slightly confused. 'OK,' he said, guessing that whatever the chief had to show him was on the walk. 'Why don't you lead the way?'

The chief used his walking stick to swing round and made his way over to the gate. Jack turned to glance over at Trevor, who was busy chatting on his mobile phone. It sounded like he was speaking in Swahili. Spying Jack, he stopped talking and waved. Jack waved back too. Then he hurried to catch up with Chief Abasi, who was already ten paces ahead.

Chapter 7:
The Find

They were only minutes from the camp when Chief Abasi started to talk. 'I am a great admirer of the GPF,' he said. 'I have been following the organization's work.' He picked up his staff and stuck it into the ground.

Jack was amazed that Chief Abasi knew about the GPF, even though he lived in the middle of the African plain. 'How do you know about us?' he asked.

'I have my sources,' the chief replied. 'Despite our simple life, I manage to stay on top of world events. Do you have any family?' he asked.

Jack was surprised by the sudden change in conversation. He paused for a moment, thinking about home. 'I do,' he said. 'My mum, my dad and my brother, Max.'

'How old is Max?' asked the chief.

'He's eleven,' said Jack. In fact, his twelfth birthday was coming up. Jack thought about how happy he'd be if he could find Max and bring him home in time for his birthday celebration.

'So, where are we going?' he asked, deciding it was best to change the subject away from Max.

'I wanted to take you to the site of the problem, so you could see it with your own eyes,' said the chief. He continued to walk ahead through the tall, dry grass. Just to the left, Jack could see eight elephants making their way across the savannah together.

Jack glanced at the temperature on his Watch Phone. It was 32°C. Feeling thirsty, he reached into the front pouch of his Book Bag and plucked out a clear plastic tube. Popping open the top, he shook out two pills and placed them on the tip of his tongue. Within seconds, they dissolved into a concentrated burst of cool water. Instantly, Jack felt refreshed. These were the GPF's Hydro Pills – the only way a secret agent could stay hydrated in conditions like this.

'That's where we are headed,' said Chief Abasi, lifting his staff and pointing to a wooden building a little way off.

Jack thought the building looked like a shed; the kind he had in his back garden at home. As they approached the building, Chief Abasi turned to Jack.

'I must warn you,' he said. 'What's inside may upset you.'

'That's all right,' said Jack, trying to sound brave.

The chief turned the handle on the shed door and pulled it wide open. He stood there waiting for Jack to take a look inside. As soon as Jack did so, he immediately noticed two things. Firstly, it didn't smell very nice. Secondly, there were lots of flies buzzing around. When his eyes finally adjusted, he knew instantly why Chief Abasi had called the GPF. Leaning against the walls were the ivory tusks of ten African elephants.

Sometimes tusks were taken from elephants that had died of natural causes. But more often elephants were gunned down and killed so that poachers could sell their tusks for money. Some people believed ivory had healing powers;

others wanted to use it for ornamental carvings. Jack turned to look at the chief, who was still outside.

'Now do you understand?' asked Chief Abasi as he shook his head in sadness.

'I do,' said Jack.

'The people who did this are not warriors,' said the chief. 'They are cowards.'

I agree,' said Jack, who couldn't believe

that anyone would
do something like
that. 'I promise I'll
find out who did
this and make sure
they never do it
again.'

   'Thank you,' said
the chief. 'Well then' – he stepped away
from the shed – 'why don't I give you
some space? I'm sure that you have work
to do.'

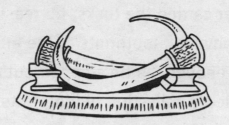

Chapter 8:
The Clues

Once Jack had his bearings, he began to look around. The first thing he studied was the tusks themselves. There was nothing unusual about them, except stamped on each with black ink was the name of a faraway country. Jack figured these were the countries buying the tusks, but there was no clue as to who was selling them off.

When he was finished, Jack turned his attention to the outside of the shed.

Whoever carried the tusks, he reasoned, would have left footprints at the entrance.

Sure enough, as he stepped outside, Jack spied a collection of footprints. One set of markings was too messy to make out; it was almost as if the person had been shuffling in the dust. The other, however, was so clear that Jack could see a squiggle on the sole of the shoe. A perfect opportunity for the GPF's Footprint Finder to do its stuff.

He grabbed the gadget from his Book Bag and turned it on by pulling on the ends of the yellow stick. Slowly, he moved the wand over the markings, giving it just enough time to register the print. Instantly, the Footprint Finder revealed the shoe's brand and size:

BOOT UNKNOWN, SIZE 11

Weird, Jack thought. The Footprint Finder almost never failed to identify a

shoe. This one must be custom-made.

He followed the footprints as they travelled from the shed to a nearby road. There they stopped at a set of four tyre marks. Luckily for Jack, he didn't need a gadget to tell him what had made these. These marks could only come from one kind of car: a four-wheel-drive truck.

Unfortunately, this was one of the most common types of vehicle on the African plain.

When Jack was finished, he joined Chief Abasi. 'I'm done,' he said.

'Did you find anything interesting?' asked the chief.

'Yeah,' said Jack, 'it looks like more than one person put the tusks in the shed. After that, they drove off in a four-wheel drive.'

'Interesting,' said the chief, considering what Jack had said. As if he was thinking about what that meant, Chief Abasi said,'I think you should meet Mr K next.'

'Mr K?' asked Jack.

'His real name is Jasper Kendall,' said the chief. 'He runs Mr K's Safari Lodge, the largest safari camp in the Maasai Mara. He and I have an arrangement of sorts,' he added. 'I let him run his business on Maasai land. In return, he lets us entertain and sell souvenirs to his guests.'

'Do you think he'll know something about the poachers?' asked Jack.

'I am not sure,' said the chief. 'But what I do know is that Jasper is extremely well-connected; he has his finger in most things going on in and around the Mara.'

'Great idea,' said Jack, who agreed that a meeting would be wise. 'Where exactly is Mr K's?'

'It's a short drive from the village,' said the chief. 'Trevor can take you and arrange for you to spend the night.'

Jack hadn't even thought about the time. He glanced at his Watch Phone. It was 5:30 p.m. Since he knew the sun set

at 7:00 p.m., he didn't have enough daylight to solve the crime that day. He was going to have to spend the night at Mr K's and carry on with his investigation in the morning.

As long as Jack stayed on a mission no longer than forty-eight hours, the GPF could return him to his bedroom at 7:31 p.m. Beyond that they'd have to fake a reason for Jack being gone. That's what they did for Max. They engineered it so he was in a 'boarding school'.

'Shall we meet up again tomorrow?' suggested Jack.

'Yes,' said Chief Abasi. 'Trevor can pick you up in the morning and bring you back to the homestead.'

'Great,' said Jack. 'That sounds like a plan.'

Just then, Trevor pulled up in a jeep. Chief Abasi looked surprised at his arrival.

'Hello there,' said Trevor, who was no longer wearing his hat. 'I borrowed a car. I figured the two of you could use a lift.'

'Stopped using the balloon, I see,' said Jack, joking with Trevor. He climbed into the back of the car, leaving the front seat for the chief. 'Aren't you coming?' he asked Chief Abasi, who was lingering behind.

'No thanks,' he said. 'I'd prefer to walk. Enjoy your visit with Mr K.' He nodded his head to say goodbye and then turned to walk in the opposite direction.

Trevor crunched the gears then slammed his foot on the accelerator. As they tore off, Jack thought about Trevor – he hoped he was a better driver than he was a balloon pilot, but held on tight to his Book Bag, just in case.

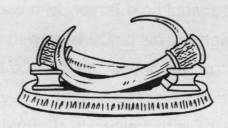

Chapter 9:
The Safari Lodge

Trevor and Jack had driven over the dusty plain for half an hour when Jack noticed a large campsite in the distance. There was an enormous wooden lodge in the middle, surrounded by dozens of oversized green tents. Around the perimeter was an electric fence. Probably, Jack thought, to keep the lions away.

'That's Mr K's,' said Trevor, pointing at the camp.

As they pulled up at the entrance, Jack spied a large sign. It was written in big, bold letters. Inside the middle of the K was a drawing of a lion.

Mr K's
SAFARI
LODGE
ALTITUDE: 5000 FT

Beside the sign stood an armed guard dressed in an olive shirt and trousers. Recognizing Trevor, he nodded and then let them pass. Trevor drove down the long track towards the lodge itself. He parked the jeep in a space marked 'reserved' and turned off the engine. Almost at the same time, a large man came out. Wearing a brown cowboy hat and a checked shirt, he looked like he belonged on the plains of Texas rather than those of Kenya.

'Hi there!' he bellowed. 'How are you doing?' He sounded like he was from South Africa. Jack guessed that Trevor had called ahead and he knew to expect them.

'So glad you could come,' he said excitedly. 'Welcome to my home. We call it Mr K's,' he added, 'after the first letter in my last name, Kendall.' He looked over at Jack with a cheesy grin. 'You get it?' he asked.

Jack looked at the man and forced a smile. There was something about Jasper

that wasn't quite right. When he glanced down at his choice in footwear, Jack was shocked. He was wearing boots made from the skin of an endangered sea turtle.

'I thought killing sea turtles for their skins was against the law,' said Jack, furrowing his brow in disapproval. He couldn't forget his duties with the GPF.

'These things?' Jasper said, brushing Jack off. 'These are so old. I've had them since before you were born!' Quickly changing the subject, he carried on. 'Why don't you come in and have a look around?' He slapped Jack on the back and led him down a gravel path towards the front door.

'Must be off,' said Trevor as he climbed into the jeep. He started up the car and began to back out. Before Jack could say goodbye, he'd sped away.

Chapter 10:
The Meal

'Now,' said Jasper, slapping Jack on the back a second time, 'let's go inside!'

He led Jack along the covered walkway and through the front door. When they entered the lobby, the first thing that caught Jack's eye was the elephant tusks. There were two decorated ivory teeth perched on a wooden stand in the corner.

Sensing that Jack was a bit stunned, Jasper explained. 'They were given to me by the previous owners. I'd never kill an elephant for its ivory.' He coughed.

Uh-oh, thought Jack. He's wearing boots from an endangered species *and* he's got two tusks proudly displayed in the front hall of his lodge. Definitely, Jack decided, a guy who needs to be watched.

As they moved into the lodge, Jack noticed several young men doing a traditional Maasai jumping dance. He knew that the Maasai showed their strength as warriors by jumping as high as they could. Remembering what Chief Abasi had said, Jack figured they were there to entertain Jasper's guests.

The two of them went through the hall and towards a wooden deck outside. Almost as soon as he stepped onto the platform, Jack was overwhelmed by the wildlife. Black and white colobus monkeys were jumping from tree to tree. A spider the size of his dad's hand sat in the

middle of its web just above Jack's head.

He walked over to the railing and looked over the edge. The deck was

perched ten metres above a river below.
There were some hippos sitting low in
the water with their ears and eyes
peeking out. A handful of baby crocodiles
were scurrying across a log as their
parents snapped up whatever food they
could.

'Why don't you have a seat?' said
Jasper, motioning for Jack to join him
at a round wooden table nearby.

Jack did just that, being careful to
watch not only his surroundings but also
his host.

'So,' said Mr K, 'Chief Abasi told me
about those tusks. Shame about the
elephants.' As he talked, he lifted his feet
and placed them on the chair next to
Jack. Since the boots weren't that far
away, Jack couldn't help but notice a
squiggly line on the soles, just like the
one he'd seen at the shed.

Jack's eyes widened. He needed to be careful. There was a chance he was sitting across from one of the poachers – if not their leader. He cleared his throat.

'Yes,' he said, trying to keep his cool. 'It's terribly upsetting.' He didn't want Jasper to know that he'd seen the boots. 'Do you know who could have done it?' he asked.

'Gosh,' said Jasper, almost sincerely. 'I

can't think of anyone.'

'Well, why do you think someone would
do it?' asked Jack.

'People round here don't make a lot of
money,' Jasper explained, 'and poaching
is one of the best ways to get it.'

Hmmm, thought Jack. Jasper wasn't
admitting to anything. Jack didn't have
enough evidence. He couldn't have him
arrested just because of his boots. For all

Jack knew, that squiggly line could be on any number of boots in the area. He was going to have to do better than that. He was going to have to catch Jasper Kendall in the act.

As Jack was thinking, a waiter came over and presented him with a plate of food. 'Jambo,' he said as he smiled down at Jack and placed the meal on the table.

'I ordered you some dinner,' said Jasper, smiling.

Jack looked down at the skewer of alternating vegetables and grey meat. 'What is it?' he asked. He'd heard that in Africa people ate all sorts of things like zebra, crocodile and wildebeest.

'An ostrich kebab,' said Mr K.

Jack eyes popped open. The last thing he wanted to do was eat *that*. Seeing Jack's reaction, Mr K roared with laughter.

'I'm actually not hungry right now,' said Jack, trying to be polite. 'Maybe I can take it back to my room.'

'Of course,' said Jasper. He motioned for the waiter to wrap Jack's dinner.

'Just one more question,' said Jack. 'Have you noticed anyone acting strangely around here?'

'No one that I can think of,' said Jasper.

'Well,' Jack said, thinking he'd got all he was going to get out of Jasper, 'I think I'd better head off to bed.' He picked up his food.

'Let me show you to your room,' said Jasper, standing to join him.

Jasper led Jack out of the dining room, through the hall and back outside.

Passing several large green tents in the compound, they arrived at one near the river bank.

'This is where you'll be sleeping

tonight,' said Jasper as he led Jack on to a small wooden deck outside the tent opening. 'I think you'll agree that our tents are pretty luxurious.'

Jack pushed back the flaps to the tent. He walked in and couldn't believe his eyes. It was as big as his bedroom at home.

'There's a hot-water bottle in your bed already,' said Jasper. 'It gets pretty cool at night. Electricity runs on a generator,' he added. 'Lights go off at eight-thirty and don't come on again until five in the morning.'

Jack looked down at his Watch Phone. It was 7:30 p.m. 'Great,' he said to Mr K, 'that'll give me an hour to do some work.'

'Sleep tight,' said Jasper as he let himself out. 'Don't let the bed bugs bite.' He gave Jack a big wink and pulled the tent flap closed behind him.

Chapter 11:
The Breakthrough

Figuring he couldn't do any more on the
case until tomorrow, Jack climbed onto
the bed and got out Max's note. He
looked at the upper-case letters again and
had a think about how to decipher the
code. During his training, the GPF had
taught him how to unscramble an
'anagram'. Anagrams were jumbled letters
that when put back into the right order
spelled a word.

He wrote out the letters again:

ABTMNNHTAUSOEETKH

Figuring the first thing Max would want to tell him was his location, he thought about places in Egypt where mummies could be found. There was the Valley of the Kings, but the letters in that word didn't match Max's code. He then thought about Thebes, the city closest to the Valley of the Kings. Sure enough, those letters were there. He crossed them out one by one.

ABTMNNYTAUSOEETKH

Then he took the letters that were left and wrote them out again:

AMNNTAUOTKH

Now, Jack reckoned, there was a pretty good chance that what remained spelled the name of the mummy near to where Max was working. Jack tried to remember all the tombs found in the Valley of the Kings. There were the tombs of Seti and Siptah. Then there were at least seven tombs belonging to Ramses. But those names didn't crack the code. And Jack couldn't remember any more. The only way he could solve this riddle was to look through his book on ancient Egypt, which unfortunately was at home.

Knowing he couldn't do anything else, Jack put his brother's letter back in his Book Bag. Popping one of the GPF's Micro Brushes into his mouth, he swirled it around, letting it brush his teeth and dissolve in his mouth. Since he didn't have any pyjamas, Jack decided to sleep in his normal clothes. He kept his Book

Bag on for safe-keeping.

After setting his Anti-Intruder Alarm,
Jack crawled under the covers and lay on
his side. Once he was comfortable, he
closed his eyes and let his mind drift off
to sleep.

Chapter 12:
The Intruder

Sometime in the early morning, Jack was woken by a strong vibration on his wrist. Uh-oh, he thought. It was his Anti-Intruder Alarm. It was telling him that there was somebody in the tent.

He lay completely still and tried to figure out who was sneaking around. Oddly enough, whoever it was barely made a sound. Usually, if someone was there, you could hear them breathe, or smell their scent. But there was nothing

like that. There was, however, a gentle
noise. It sounded like it was coming from
above Jack's head.

Sssssssss.

Sssssssss.

It was coming closer.

Sssssssss.

Sssssssss.

Thinking he had an idea what it was,
Jack slowly rose to a kneeling position
and turned on his Everglo Light. A bright
beam shot from his Watch Phone and lit
the entire room.

At first Jack didn't notice it because it
was the same colour as his green tent.

But when he did, he nearly jumped with shock.

It was an African boomslang, one of the deadliest snakes in the world, and it was hanging from a light in the middle of Jack's room.

Chapter 13:
The Idea

Before Jack could do anything, the snake had coiled itself to within one metre of his face. As Jack looked up, he stared into the snake's eyes. They were black and cold. Boomslangs were hemotoxic, which meant they injected a poison that could make you bleed to death. And they were aggressive – one move from Jack and the snake would strike.

Since boomslangs were tree-dwelling snakes, the only way Jack could save himself was to pretend he was a tree. He slowed his breathing down and sat totally still.

Closing his eyes, Jack waited. The first thing he felt was the snake's cold body brushing against his nose. Then he felt it slide across his face. Slithering over his right shoulder, the snake made its way around his Book Bag and down the length of his back. Although it was travelling fairly quickly for a boomslang, it wasn't quick enough as far as Jack was concerned. It took all his energy and concentration not to move. But he had to

remain still, or the snake would bite.

Finally, Jack felt the snake slide off him and onto the mattress. As soon as he heard its heavy body thump onto the floor, he opened his eyes and looked around. The front flap to the tent had been left open. When he went to bed it was closed. It was looking like the snake being there was no accident.

He looked over his shoulder and spied the snake's tail going under his bed. Thinking this was a perfect opportunity to escape, Jack carefully stood up and, using the beam from the Everglo Light, leaped as far as he could away from the bed. He hurried to the opening of the tent and stopped to look back. The boomslang was coming out from under the bed. Not wanting to come to face to face with the creature again, Jack quickly headed out through the flap.

Now that he was outside, Jack decided the safest place for him was the lodge. Although the tents were dark, the main lodge was lit throughout the night. With the beam of his Everglo Light guiding him, he made his move. Just to his left, he could hear hippos burrowing themselves in the bank. From somewhere above came the strange sound of an unknown animal. Jack reckoned he'd seen enough of the local wildlife for one night, and hurried towards the main building as quickly as he could.

Chapter 14:
The Transfer

'Jack!' said a voice from up ahead. Thanks to the glow of his torch, Jack could see that it was Jasper Kendall heading towards him. 'What are you doing here?' he asked, seeming surprised. 'It's a bit early to be out and about, isn't it?'

Yeah right, thought Jack, who was thinking it was more than a coincidence that Jasper was up this early too. Maybe he was the one who'd put the snake in Jack's tent. Not wanting to betray his private thoughts, Jack just shrugged. 'I wanted to use the lights in the main lodge to do some work.'

'I see,' said Jasper. He didn't seem convinced by Jack's excuse. 'Why don't I take you there?' he said, leading Jack by the arm. 'Shall I call Trevor and tell him that you'll be ready . . . a bit earlier than expected?'

'That would be nice,' said Jack.

They soon reached the main building and Mr K called Trevor. It wasn't long before he arrived. He pulled up in the darkened car park. After all, it was only 6:00 a.m.

'Morning,' Trevor said. 'I was thinking I'd take you on a safari drive. It's too early to see the old man anyway,' he said, meaning Chief Abasi. 'He's probably still asleep. But the animals, on the other hand, are just starting to wake up.'

Jack thought that was a great idea. Any opportunity to learn about the animals, especially the elephants, could only help with the investigation. He also wanted to search for clues that would tie Jasper Kendall to the crime.

'Excellent idea,' said Jack as he climbed into the front seat. He was impressed by Trevor's new Land Rover. He'd ridden in the same kind once with his dad at a local motor show. 'Nice car,' he said.

'Thanks,' said Trevor. 'I got it in Mombasa.'

Jack turned in his seat and looked at Mr K, who was waiting at the edge of the car park. He waved goodbye and gave Jack one of his cheesy grins. I'll get you, thought Jack as he waved back. It's just a matter of time.

Chapter 15:
The Lions' Den

They'd driven for half an hour in darkness when Trevor piped up. 'There's a place nearby where you can see the sunrise and watch the animals,' he said.

'Sounds great,' said Jack, who was looking forward to a break. After all, he'd had a stressful morning.

After a few minutes, Trevor shifted the truck down a gear. 'This is the place I told you about,' he said as the Land Rover began to climb a steep hill. The truck rocked back and forth as it made its way over some jagged rocks. 'You'll love the view from up here.' He sounded very excited.

When the truck heaved over the ridge, Trevor drove onto a flatter piece of land. With the sun beginning to rise, Jack could make out some trees lining the top of the hill. Dotting the ground were what looked like small- to medium-sized rocks. Then Trevor put the truck into neutral.

As Jack looked around, he noticed something odd. There weren't any animals here. What was Trevor thinking? he said to himself. Then he heard what sounded like a lion's yawn.

Squinting, Jack could just make out some larger shapes underneath the trees. As the sun's light grew brighter by second, things became clearer. There were six adult lions lying down on their bellies. Four of them were female; two were male. Jack knew this because two had magnificent manes of hair. He wouldn't have been so worried if it hadn't been for the fact that the Land Rover didn't have any doors on its sides.

'Trevor,' said Jack, not wanting to sound scared, 'isn't this a bit risky? I'd like to see some wild animals,' he added, 'but maybe not lions that are *this* close.'

Trevor turned to him. 'Get out,' he said. But he didn't say it kindly; he said it with a sinister snarl.

'What?' said Jack, who wasn't sure he'd heard Trevor correctly.

Trevor opened the glove box in front of Jack. He reached in and pulled out a knife in a brown leather sheath. As he slid the cover off with his other hand, he glared at Jack.

'You heard me,' he growled. 'Get out! And if you don't,' he added, 'I'll have to use this.' Trevor waved the knife in Jack's face so he could see its razor-sharp edge.

Jack was stunned. What was going on? Where was the friendly Trevor he knew? And *why* was he holding a knife in Jack's face?

'I've been collecting those tusks for weeks,' Trevor explained. 'And then Chief Abasi has to go and find them on one of his little "walks". Now, I have to find more ivory,' he explained. 'My Far Eastern buyers are desperate for their goods, and I don't need the likes of you getting in the way.'

Jack was almost speechless with surprise. 'But I thought—' he said, thinking about Jasper Kendall and the boot prints he'd found at the shed.

'What, that Jasper Kendall had something to do with it?' Trevor snarled. 'That guy couldn't pick his nose if it weren't for me! I knew a little busy-body like you would come sniffing around the shed if it was ever found,' he explained, 'so I put Jasper's boots on and made some nice tracks. Looks like it worked. Otherwise you wouldn't be here with me.'

Jack thought back to when he'd first met Trevor. Trevor had acted like he was a bit of a clown . . . the floppy hat, his wacky way of piloting the balloon, the way he talked. That was all just a trick to make Jack think he was a nice guy, not a cold-hearted ivory poacher!

'I tried to get rid of you last night,' Trevor went on, 'but somehow you managed to escape. This time,' he added with a snigger, 'I think the lions will do a better job.'

Of course, Jack thought. Trevor must have snuck back into the camp and put the snake in his tent. It would have been very easy for him to do. After all, they were used to seeing him around Mr K's because he worked for him.

Jack didn't have much time. He pulled his thoughts together. 'But how can you kill innocent animals?' he said, trying to distract Trevor. As he spoke, he took what looked like a coin out of his pocket and let it drop to the floor of the Land Rover.

'There's only one simple answer to that question,' said Trevor. 'Money . . . Now get out!'

Jack thought about his options. Unfortunately for him there wasn't a gadget that could get him out of a situation involving a knife. There was only one thing to do, and that was to climb out of the car and take his chances with the lions.

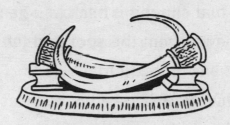

Chapter 16:
The Tree

With the sun nearly up, Jack could finally see what he was up against. The lions were now standing on all fours. They were watching him as he got out of the truck.

'Trevor,' said Jack as he stepped out onto the dirt, 'I'm warning you. Don't do this. African elephants are already endangered. Killing more will just make matters worse.'

Trevor laughed one last dramatic laugh – he didn't care at all. He revved the engine and slipped it back into gear, then peeled away from the spot and left Jack without any protection.

'*ROOOOAAARR!*'

Quickly, Jack turned round to see one of the male lions licking his chops. The females were gathering together. Jack knew that lions hunted in the early morning, which meant that they were probably looking at Jack as easy food. He didn't have much time to act. He was going to have to get out of there before they attacked.

Taking off his Book Bag, Jack crouched down. The female lions were beginning to surround him, since they did all the hunting. With animals on all sides, there was only one gadget that could help Jack.

The GPF's Power Pogo was a pogo stick like no other. With one bounce, it could catapult you up to five metres high.

Jack grabbed the life-saving gadget, strapped his Book Bag back on and placed his hands and one foot on the Power Pogo. He looked at the lions. The female lions were inching closer while the male lions were waiting patiently under the trees.

'ROOOOAAARR!'

Like lightning, the lionesses sprang into action, pushing with their strong hind legs to leap forward. They were charging at top speed in an attempt to bring Jack down. Quickly, Jack lifted his other foot and jumped onto the pogo stick for its first bounce. When it hit the ground, it flew up into the air.

BOING!

One of the lion's paws just missed Jack's feet as he rocketed into the sky, then came crashing back to the ground. Luckily for Jack, he landed just to the right

of the pride of lions, who were scrambling to reach him.

BOING!

This time he sprang even further. One more time, thought Jack, and he'd be next to the trees.

BOING!

The Power Pogo thrust him towards an acacia tree. As he came down, he grabbed onto one of its branches and held on. His feet were dangling down. The Power Pogo fell to the dusty ground, almost hitting one of the male lions on the head.

'ROOOOAAARR!'

The lion wasn't happy. Using the strength in his arms, Jack pulled himself up onto a branch. Perched there for safety, he glanced down at the lions below. Their 'easy' breakfast had completely disappeared. Jack smiled.

Things were finally going his way.

Taking a moment, he remembered what Trevor had said. He needed more ivory. Guessing that's where Trevor was off to now, Jack looked at his Watch Phone and punched a few buttons. The Transponder that he'd dropped in Trevor's car was showing a location just ten miles away. Since the blinking light wasn't moving, Jack started to worry.

He had to get to Trevor before he killed another elephant. He looked over towards the other side of tree in which he was sitting. There was a gentle drop from the hill to the savannah. Peering through the branches at the lions, he saw that they had given up on catching him. The pride was heading somewhere else in search of food. Lowering himself down, he collected his gadget, packed it away and scrambled through some bushes to the top of the slope. He slid down it towards the flatter land below. Perfect terrain, Jack thought, for one of his favourite gadgets. It was the GPF's Flyboard and it was waiting for him in his Book Bag.

Chapter 17:
The Confrontation

After snapping the Flyboard together, Jack hopped on. Punching the 'air' button on his Watch Phone, the jets fired up and he and the Flyboard took off. Given the distance and the speed he was travelling, Jack worked out he would arrive at the Land Rover within moments.

He soon saw Trevor's truck ahead. It looked as if he was just in time. Directly across from the truck was a family of elephants. They were bumping into trees

and grasping at branches with their
trunks. Trevor was standing by the vehicle
with another man. It looked like the
waiter from Mr K's lodge – the one who
had served Jack his ostrich kebab. So
that's Trevor's accomplice, thought Jack.
That's who left the set of messy footprints
at the shed.

The two men were wearing hunter's vests and pointing their guns towards one of the female elephants.

'No!' screamed Jack, urging the Flyboard to go faster.

But Trevor and the other man couldn't hear him; he was still half a mile away. They leaned their ears on the guns and looked through the sights.

'Stop!' yelled Jack.

At that last shout, Trevor must have heard him, because he lifted his head and looked in Jack's direction. By the time both men had registered Jack's arrival, he was nearly there.

'You?' snarled Trevor, clearly unhappy to see that Jack had escaped a second time. 'What are you doing here?' he yelled. 'Go away! We have some business to do.'

'No you don't,' said Jack. 'I'm not going to let you kill these elephants!'

'Oh yeah?' said Trevor, swinging his gun so that it was now pointing at Jack.

Jack flinched.

'*Hapana!*' the other man yelled in Swahili, aiming his gun at Jack too. The female elephant sensed the danger and was leading her family in the other direction.

As Trevor gripped his gun tightly, ready to fire, Jack pulled his Lava Laser out of his bag. Even though it looked like an ordinary pencil, the GPF's Lava Laser was powerful enough to make metal burn as hot as lava, so that whoever was touching it would have to drop it.

Trevor put his finger on the trigger. Jack fired the Lava Laser. A ray of light shot out of the gadget and struck the metal on Trevor's gun. Almost instantly, it started to glow orange with heat, burning Trevor's hands.

'Owwww!' he yelled in agony, dropping the hot metal object.

'*Hapana!*' the Kenyan man yelled, lowering his face to his gun. He was about to fire.

But Jack and the Lava Laser got him too.

'Arghhhh!' he howled, shaking his hands and trying to cool them. Jack guessed that a cry of pain sounded the same in Swahili as it did in English.

Realizing that they weren't going to kill either Jack or the elephants, the two men dropped in their seats. They were going to start up their truck. Trevor tried to turn the key in the ignition, but his hands were too sore and blistered to touch a thing.

'Arrgh!' he yelled, obviously disgusted with what was happening.

Panicked and desperate, the two men jumped out. They started to run in different directions. Jack reached into his pocket and pulled out his Transformation Dust. He opened the packet and directed the Flyboard over to the waiter from Mr K's lodge.

'Rhinoceros,' Jack said as he blew some of the dust onto the man's face.

'*Kifaru?*' the waiter said, repeating the word for rhinoceros in Swahili. As the dust flew into his face, he coughed, spat and shook his head. Almost instantly, he was transformed into one of the most hunted and endangered African animals – the black rhino. Jack then sped over to Trevor, who was sprinting as fast as he could, but not fast enough.

'Please don't!' Trevor screamed as he looked at his accomplice and realized what Jack was about to do. 'Noooo!'

'Elephant,' said Jack as he blew the dust. On that very spot, Trevor was turned

into a two-ton female elephant. He lifted
his trunk and blew a sound of fury.

'Now,' said Jack, pleased with himself.
'Let's see how *you* like being a hunted
animal.'

Although Jack would have loved to keep
them that way for ever, he knew the GPF's
Transformation Dust would only last an
hour. No problem, he thought. It was a

clever enough way to catch the poachers *and* teach them a lesson at the same time.

Jack phoned the Kenyan police, who arrived fairly quickly, but not soon enough for either Trevor or the waiter, who were being sniffed at by a pack of hyenas.

Once the criminals had changed back into their human forms, the police officers arrested them and hauled them off.

'You're going to pay for this, kid!' yelled Trevor as the van door shut behind him.

No, thought Jack to himself. *You're* the one who's going to pay.

Chapter 18:
The Find

Now that the bad guys were locked up, it was time to pay a visit to Chief Abasi. After all, Jack was supposed to meet him this morning and he was already late.

He jumped on his Flyboard and headed for the homestead. As he zoomed towards the gate of the Maasai village, Chief Abasi came out of a hut to greet him.

'Hello, Jack,' he said, using his stick to walk over. 'Has anything happened since we last spoke?'

'You wouldn't believe the morning I've had!' said Jack. 'I was nearly bitten by a poisonous boomslang and mauled by a pack of lions!'

Chief Abasi eyes widened at the news.

'But everything is all right now,' Jack explained. 'I caught Trevor and a waiter from Mr K's trying to kill more elephants. They were the poachers responsible for those tusks in the shed.'

Chief Abasi wobbled on his feet before taking a step back. He was obviously in a state of shock. 'I can't believe this,' he said. 'Trevor was a trusted friend of the Maasai people.'

'Unfortunately, I don't think Trevor was anybody's friend,' said Jack. 'He pretended to be nice so nobody would suspect him of the crime. But Trevor's locked up now, so he'll have plenty of time to think about what he's done.'

Chief Abasi shook his head. 'Well then,' he said to Jack, 'we owe you and the GPF a great deal of thanks. You've rid our area of some nasty poachers and the elephants here in Kenya will be safer thanks to your efforts.'

'No problem,' said Jack, who was pleased with himself. 'I'm just happy I could help.' He held out his hand. 'If there are any more problems, give me a call.'

'I will,' said the chief, putting his hand in Jack's. 'Be safe in your travels. And to help guide you, I would like to give you a gift.' Chief Abasi left Jack for a moment and walked to his hut.

When he returned, he had a red beaded necklace in his hands. 'This is for good luck,' he said, handing it to Jack. 'And for the luck of your family.'

Little did the chief know, thought Jack, how much luck the Stalwart family actually needed. As he looked down at the necklace, he thought about his brother, Max.

Jack picked it up and smiled. 'Thank you,' he said as he placed it around his neck. 'I'll treasure it always.' He waved goodbye to the chief and stepped onto his Flyboard.

Leaving the homestead behind, he flew across the hot plains and stopped near a cluster of bushes. He packed his gadget away and, after pushing a few buttons on his Watch Phone, closed his eyes and yelled, 'Off to England!' Within moments Jack was transported home to his bedroom.

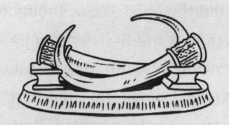

Chapter 19:
The Breakthrough

As soon as he arrived, Jack grabbed the book on ancient Egypt from his bookcase and sat down with it and his brother's note. He flicked through the pages and found one with a list of all the tombs in the Valley of the Kings, then laid out what was left of the code again:

AMNNTAUOTKH

Jack compared the tomb names with the letters in the code. The first name on the list was Merenptah, but that didn't work. Scrolling down, he tried to match every name with the anagram, but nothing seemed to fit. By the time he got to the last name, he didn't hold out much hope. Jack wrote out the letters anyway. After all, King Tut was the most famous mummy in the world.

As he was writing, he realized that nearly every letter fitted with the anagram from Max's note.

TUTANKHAMON

The only problem was that in the book Tutankhamun was spelled with a 'u' instead of the 'o' that was in Max's code. Drat, thought Jack. Maybe he was wrong. Maybe the letters spelled another mummy's name.

But it was so close. Perhaps, wondered Jack, there was another spelling. He knew this was common when it came to ancient names for people and places. Feeling excited, he raced over to his computer and punched the name Tutankhamun into the search field. Three different spellings for the famous boy king showed up.

One of them was spelled with an 'o'.

Jack looked down at the necklace that Chief Abasi had given him. 'Thanks,' he whispered to the man who had given him the necklace and his incredible good luck.

TUTANKHAMON

It was a perfect match.